PEPPERMINT FAIRIES

By Evelyn Norton

Illustrated by Mariness Rivera

Special Thanks To:

My Mommy for helping me
with hard decisions

Do you know about Peppermint Fairies? They have a peppermint patch. You can find it right in the middle of town. Everyone shares it, and everyone works really hard. But peppermint fairies don't plant seeds, they plant…

Pixie dust! The pixie dust comes from a very special, very rare...

...Flower. It only blooms on Christmas Eve. As the flower opens up the peppermint fairies gather the dust and take it back to Peppermint Village to plant it in the peppermint patch.

The pixie dust is planted in the ground, watered, sung to, and loved.

Then something starts to happen very quickly.

Out from the ground grows...

Candy cane flowers!
Inside those very unusual
flowers are...

Peppermints! The peppermint fairies work quickly to gather the peppermints. They have an important job to do.

In the next village over, the people are already gathering together around the town Christmas tree. They hold hands around the tree and sing as they wait for it to...

Rain peppermints!

As the villagers hold out their hands and catch
a teeny tiny fairy size peppermint...

It grows! Pop! Into a very normal, human sized peppermint.

These are the best peppermints of all! They are very special. The village people take these peppermints home and...

Plant them! From the soil they came and to the soil they go.

Plop, plop, plop! Into the neat little rows behind every house. And with a little water and a song or two, the people from one village down anxiously watch and wait for...

Peppermint pumpkins starting to grow! First comes a little sprout, all bright green and stretching up, up, up. Then the sprout grows into a vine, and this is the exciting part…

A small little peppermint pumpkin can be seen starting to grow between two leaves!
Watch carefully and you will see how it grows!
So big! So wonderfully… striped!

It is a peppermint pumpkin after all, that came from a magic peppermint, that came from a candy cane flower, that grew from pixie dust.

Oh what a sight! Oh what a smell! The children are setting the table. The moms are preparing the kitchen. The dads are collecting the peppermint pumpkins.

For you see, the peppermint pumpkins are the perfect ingredient for...

Peppermint pumpkin pie!

About Me

Hi, I'm Evelyn, and I'm 7 years old! In 2019, my Mommy read a book to me about a famous author. The book mentioned a trip that this author took to see orphanages in Eastern Europe and the charity that she built as a result from that trip. I wanted to donate to the charity so I started making little handmade books and selling them for $1 each. I even got some friends at school to join me and we created a club and called ourselves "Kid's

Company." When we earned $10, my Mommy would go online and donate the money to this charity. We would print out the confirmation page and give it to those who bought books from us as a sort of receipt to show that we were keeping our word and donating the money like we said we would. I wanted to sell more books and reach more people, so my Mommy and Daddy did some research and we all decided that the best way to do this was to self-publish one of my books and sell it online. A part of the money that we get from each book sold goes straight to the charity.

If you want to know about the charity and how it helps orphans, find me on social media at:

@BooksByEvelynRose

LET'S HELP THE WORLD!